A tough choice

The Archangel of Compassion pursed her lips. "All right, little angel, what is it: should I ask another little angel to do this task so that you can enjoy the rest of field day, or do you want to help Molly?"

The Little Angel of Compassion looked back at her team. The egg event was almost over—just one more person to go. Then there was the three-legged race. And the water balloon toss. And so many other wonderful things.

The Little Angel of Compassion blew on her harmonica as loud as she could. Her teammates looked back at her. She waved good-bye. There would be other field days.

Aladdin
Angelwings
№. 13

Left Out

Donna Jo Napoli

Aladdin Paperbacks

New York London Toronto Sydney Singapore

Thank you to all my family,
Brenda Bowen, Karen Riskin, and Richard Tchen

First Aladdin Paperbacks edition September 2000

Text copyright © 2000 by Donna Jo Napoli

Aladdin Paperbacks
An imprint of Simon & Schuster Children's Publishing Division
1230 Avenue of the Americas
New York, NY 10020

The text for this book was set in Minister Light and Cheltenham.

Printed and bound in the United States of America
2 4 6 8 10 9 7 5 3 1

Library of Congress Catalog Card Number: 00-106485
ISBN 0-689-83971-5

If you've ever really been embarrassed by a family member, this book's for you.

Aladdin

Angelwings

№ 13

Left Out

Angel Talk

The little angels crowded together, waiting for their turn in the races.

Every detail of the day was perfect so far: The archangels had prepared a feast for midday, tons of little angels had come to play, and even the weather was right—balmy.

The Little Angel of Compassion carefully balanced an egg on a spoon and held the spoon between her teeth. The goal of this event was to go as fast as possible all the way to a post on the other side of the field and back again without dropping the egg. If it were up to her, she'd have gone slowly—one step with each breath—rather than risk breaking the egg. But she couldn't let her team down. She clenched her teeth and took long, smooth strides, all the way across the field, all the way back. Yay! She passed her egg to the next in line.

"Good work, little angel," said the Archangel of Compassion.

"Thank you." The Little Angel of Compassion pulled her harmonica out of her pocket and swung it round and round on its chain. "I don't really understand, though, why we do this race with eggs. If we drop them, the poor chicks inside die."

"Those eggs don't hold baby chicks. They're not fertilized."

"Oh, good," said the little angel.

"I was wondering . . . how much are you looking forward to the rest of the events in this field day?" asked the Archangel of Compassion.

The little angel looked up at her curiously. "You have a task for me, don't you?"

"Mmmhmm."

The Little Angel of Compassion touched the feathers at the edges of her wings. Each feather had been rewarded to her for helping a child who needed to learn compassion. The little angel loved all her feathers, but there was still a big bare spot in the center of each wing. She had a long way to go before those wings would be entirely feathered and she'd hear the bell that announced her passage from being a little angel to being an archangel. "Is it worth a lot of feathers? Enough to earn my wings?"

The archangel gave a sympathetic smile. "I'm not sure. But I do know this girl needs you."

The little angel looked wistfully back at the races. "Could it wait till tomorrow?"

"Every day we wait, the problem grows bigger."

"I'll be the only little angel to miss the rest of field day," said the Little Angel of Compassion.

"No, you won't. Look." The Archangel of Compassion pointed to one little angel sitting alone, watching the races from a distance.

"But she chose not to race," said the little

angel. "She quit on her last angel task because she was lazy. She's too lazy to even join the race."

"How do you know it was laziness that made her quit?" asked the archangel.

"Everyone knows."

The archangel gave a little tsk. "Has anyone invited her to join a team?"

"Of course not. She wants to be alone."

"And how do you know that?" asked the archangel.

"She hasn't talked to anyone for a week."

The archangel pursed her lips. Then she lifted her eyebrows. "All right, little angel, what is it: Should I ask another little angel to do this task so that you can enjoy the rest of field day, or do you want to help Molly?"

"She really needs help?" asked the little angel.

"Really."

The little angel looked back at her team. The egg event was almost over—just one more person to go. Then there was the three-legged race. And the water-balloon toss. And so many other wonderful things.

The Little Angel of Compassion blew on her harmonica as loud as she could. Her teammates looked back at her. She waved good-bye. There would be other field days.

Already her mind was racing on to the task ahead. Molly needed her. And, who knew? Maybe after Molly learned compassion, a bell would ring.

Party

Molly walked toward the girls over by the swing set.

Celia looked up at her and said loudly, "Oh, hi, Molly."

The other three girls stopped talking and turned to face Molly. "Hi."

Molly knew immediately that they'd been talking about something they didn't want her to hear. She was used to that. Ever since her big sister had a baby, people hushed when she came near, and she knew they had been talking about her. Even before the baby came, when Amanda was pregnant, they did that. But Celia was Molly's friend. How could Celia talk behind her back? Molly lifted her chin and smiled. "What's up?" she asked, as though nothing was wrong.

6

"Hey," said Celia.

"Let's go get a ball from the equipment shed and play basketball," said Teresa.

"Yeah," said another girl. They ran ahead, leaving Celia and Molly alone for a moment.

"What were you talking about?" asked Molly.

"Nothing."

"Oh, sure. That's why everyone stopped when I came over." Molly stooped and brushed dirt off her shoe. She stood up again. "I wouldn't say anything behind your back, Celia. No matter what."

"It wasn't about your sister or the baby, I swear," said Celia.

"Then why can't I know?"

"Oh, okay." Celia looked away. "You know how the town pool is opening for the season on Saturday? Well, there's going to be a party at the pool."

"A swimming party? I love to swim."

"But you can't come," said Celia.

7

"Who says?"

"Beth's mother." Celia finally looked at Molly again. "She's the one in charge of refreshments. And you know how she is."

Molly knew, all right. Beth hadn't been allowed to invite Molly to her birthday party last fall. Beth's mother told Beth that girls who got pregnant in high school weren't nice and that Molly was probably going to turn out just like her big sister. And Beth told Molly. Beth stood there on the sidewalk in front of school and said those things. Molly's mouth went sour now, just remembering. "The town pool doesn't belong to Beth's mother. She can't keep me from coming and swimming. I can swim all day long if I want."

Celia touched Molly's sleeve. "Don't do that. You'll just feel awful."

"Maybe I'll do it and maybe I won't. And I think basketball is boring." Molly turned around and ran back to the swing sets. But Beth, of all people, was standing in the line.

So Molly ran past the swings to the ugly old sycamore tree and sat at the bottom with her back against the trunk. She didn't like basketball. In fact, she was lousy at all ball games. But it was fun to play just to be with everyone. She closed her eyes.

Amanda had done this to her. Amanda had ruined her life.

A long, sweet note filled the air. Molly didn't know who was playing the harmonica and she didn't want to know. She put her hands over her ears and thought of nothing.

Angel Talk

I don't understand," said the Little Angel of Compassion. "You said I was supposed to help Molly, but it's Beth who needs to learn compassion. And Beth's mother."

"You'll have your hands full teaching Molly," said the Archangel of Compassion.

The little angel took out her harmonica from one pocket and a soft cloth from the other. She polished the harmonica. "You can't mean that you want me to teach Molly to feel compassion for the other girls. They're the mean ones, not Molly. They can't blame Molly for something her sister did."

"Oh, little angel, the task grows bigger and

bigger. But start with Molly, okay? She does need you."

"I'll try. I don't know what I can do to help her. But I'll try."

The Swan

"Molly? Is that you?" Amanda called.

Molly slipped off her backpack and walked into the kitchen. She knew Amanda wanted her to help with Clayton, but so what? He was Amanda's baby; he was Amanda's responsibility. She poured herself a glass of milk and searched through the cupboards for cookies. Only a box of Fig Newtons was left, and someone had ripped the plastic wrapping, so they were dried out and hard. That was probably Amanda's doing—she ate a lot of cookies at night, staying up playing her dumb music.

Molly rested her hand on the edge of the sink and drank her milk. Then she washed the glass and turned around.

"Hi. Didn't you hear me call?" Amanda

stood there with Clayton on her hip. Clayton grinned and squealed with delight when he saw Molly. "I've got to go shopping," said Amanda. "I kept Clayton up past his nap time just so he'd be ready to sleep when you came home. So will you keep an ear open for him while I'm gone?"

"You know Mom said I'm too young to baby-sit." Molly walked past them, ignoring Clayton's outstretched hand. She didn't understand why the baby liked her so much. She didn't like him. His ears stuck out, and he drooled everywhere, and he was always pulling her hair. "Wait till Mom and Dad get home from work."

Amanda followed her into the living room. "You won't actually be baby-sitting. Mrs. Gemelli is home, and if Clayton wakes up, you're supposed to call her and she'll come over to take care of him. That way I don't have to pay her while he sleeps. You don't have to do anything at all." Amanda kissed

Clayton on top of the head. "Ready for bed, sweetie?"

Clayton wriggled madly. He didn't look ready at all.

"Mrs. Gemelli can't take care of a baby. All she can do is sit on the couch and read." Molly should know. For years Mom and Dad had paid the old lady to be there when Molly came home from school. In fact, it was only because Amanda didn't go to school anymore that Mrs. Gemelli wasn't here now. "Plus Mom and Dad will get mad if you leave me alone."

"Mrs. Gemelli won't really have to do anything. She's just backup. In case. And you take care of yourself fine," said Amanda. "Please."

"I can't hear him if I'm outside playing," said Molly.

"But you always do your homework after school," said Amanda. "By the time you're through, I'll be back and you can go out to play until dinner."

"Sometimes I like to play right after school," said Molly. "Besides, shopping isn't important."

"Wow, you're certainly a grump today. I need you to do this, Molly. I need a new outfit."

Stupid Amanda—she'd been working at the grocery checkout counter on weekends for the past month and now she was going to waste her money on an outfit. "What for? So you can go try to look pretty for some dumb boy?"

Amanda's face went blotchy pink and red, as though she was going to cry. "This has nothing to do with looking pretty. I can't fit into my old clothes—and I need to look good for tomorrow."

"Stop eating all the cookies and you won't be so fat."

"I work hard to be patient with you, Molly—I'm all on my own here—and all you do is pick on me. What did I ever do to you? Forget it. Just forget I ever asked." Amanda ran up the stairs.

Molly opened her backpack. She really did like to finish her homework before playing. But how could she now, after she'd told Amanda she wanted to play first? And, worse, how could she go play? The only person to play with was Celia, and Molly didn't want to be with Celia now. Molly didn't want to be with anyone.

Clayton was crying.

Molly could hear the shower. She spread her math homework on the table.

Clayton was still crying.

What kind of mother was Amanda that she'd take a shower with her baby crying like that?

Molly quietly crept up the stairs and peeked into Clayton's room. He lay on his back and reached through the bars of the crib toward the yellow swan on top of his dresser. Aunt Barbara had brought that swan yesterday. But it had a little collar around its neck with a bell on it, and Amanda said Clayton couldn't have it till he was past the stage of putting everything in his mouth. She didn't want him to swallow the bell.

Molly inspected the crib. Everything looked fine. Clayton was safe. He cried only because he wanted the stupid swan. Molly could try singing to him, but sometimes singing excited Clayton instead of putting him to sleep. And, oh, there was that har-monica again—playing one long note that got softer and softer. Was Molly imagining it? But Clayton seemed to hear it, too. He stopped crying and stared at the ceiling.

Molly went back downstairs to do her math.

Angel Talk

"Clayton's cute," said the Little Angel of Compassion.

"And he seems to like your harmonica."

"He does, doesn't he? Maybe I'll play him lullabies. Babies love lullabies."

"What do you love about your harmonica?" asked the archangel.

"Well, I can play the right note for any moment." The little angel held her harmonica in her palm and looked at it. "I can make it match someone's sadness or match someone's joy. And when they hear it, they understand how they feel. And so do other people."

"It's a good instrument for an angel of compassion, then," said the archangel.

"Yup. I think I'll play 'Brahms' Lullaby' for Clayton."

"Are you forgetting about Molly?" asked the Archangel of Compassion.

"Molly's sticking up for herself pretty well," said the little angel. "She was right: She shouldn't have to help out with Clayton. And who cares if Amanda gets a new outfit or not? I bet she's the one who let the Fig Newtons get ruined."

"Wow, you sound just like Molly."

"I'm supposed to be on her side, aren't I?" The little angel swung her harmonica around on its chain. "I understand Molly. I understand her anger."

The Archangel of Compassion caught the harmonica in midair. She leaned over and blew into it. A shrill note came out.

"Do you know how to play?" asked the little angel.

"Only a little. I just wanted you to hear it for a moment. I wanted you to hear your anger."

"It was ugly," the little angel said slowly.

"That's what I think, too."

"I don't want Molly to be full of shrill anger."

"Then work on that first." The Archangel of Compassion placed the harmonica in the little angel's hand. "Getting rid of anger is a good starting point on the road to compassion."

The Bathroom

"I missed you yesterday afternoon." Celia hopped off the bottom step of the school bus and ran to the sidewalk. She turned around and waited for Molly. "And I wanted to sit near you on the bus this morning. Why'd you sit beside Harry? He makes all those funny little grunts."

"Harry's not so bad." Molly walked briskly.

"What's the hurry?" Celia ran to catch up. "You're mad at me, aren't you?"

"Of course not."

"Yes, you are. You're mad because you can't go to the swim party. But that's not my fault."

"I know that." Molly walked faster. "You don't have to go, though."

"Not go? Be fair, Molly. It's a big deal. All

21

the girls are going to have a sleep over at Beth's house afterward. Look, we can play before the party. We can spend all morning together."

"I might be busy Saturday morning."

"Doing what?"

"I just remembered something important. I'll see you later." Molly walked fast toward the school building. The happy screams and shouts from the playground followed her into the foyer, but once she went through the big swinging doors into the wide corridor, everything was silent. She hadn't really remembered anything—she just wanted to get away from Celia's question, away from the image of all the girls having a wonderful sleep over at Beth's house.

So what now? Molly felt conspicuous in this empty hall. Children weren't allowed in the school building until the first bell rang unless they had to use the bathroom or see the nurse. The normal bathroom for her grade was up on the south wing of the second floor. But there was a closer bathroom right across the hall from the library. Molly ducked into it.

The floors shone clean and bright. Molly tiptoed over to the last stall and closed the door behind her. She'd just wait here till the bell rang. It couldn't be that long. The smell of pine-scented disinfectant made her nose prickle.

Someone came running in. The person burst into the first stall and banged around. Molly heard a little gasp. She got down on her knees and looked under the partition across the bottoms of the stalls. Someone dropped her underwear on the floor. It fell with a wet slap. Then she picked it up with the tips of her index finger and thumb and went out of the stall.

Molly opened her stall door quietly and watched as Sasha stuffed the wet underwear into the trash by the sink. Sasha was Beth's best friend.

Sasha's eyes met Molly's in the mirror. She jumped around. "What are you doing here?"

Molly shrugged. A high, clear note of pain rang in her ears.

Sasha's eyes got glassy. "I have a condition. That's what the doctor says. I'll outgrow it."

"Sure," said Molly.

"Don't tell anyone."

"I won't."

"Please." Sasha left.

Molly thought about Sasha off and on for the rest of the day. She watched her sit primly with her knees together and her skirt pulled over them at recess. She watched her walk with careful little steps in the lunchroom. How awful it would be to go through the day in a skirt with no underwear on.

But no one knew, at least. No one but Molly. So it wasn't as bad as having an unwed mother for a sister. Not nearly as bad.

Angel Talk

oo bad it wasn't Beth instead of Sasha," said the Little Angel of Compassion.

The Archangel of Compassion looked shocked. "What on earth can you be thinking of? Are you wishing evil on Beth?"

"No, I didn't mean it that way. Only, if it had been Beth, then Beth would have seen what a nice person Molly is, to keep her secret. She'd have talked her mother into letting Molly come to the swim party on Saturday."

"Maybe. But there's no point thinking about it, because it was Sasha, not Beth. And not going to the party on Saturday is the least of Molly's problems."

"I think the party is a pretty big problem," said the little angel. "I'd feel terrible if I got left out like that."

"It is a pretty big problem," said the archangel. "But it's only a problem right now. A year from now Molly might not even remember the party. And ten years from now she certainly won't. But she has to deal with her family for a long, long time."

"Who cares about ten years from now, or even one year from now? Molly has to face these children every day right now. And now is all she knows."

The Archangel of Compassion smoothed the little angel's robe. "You're right. I've been seeing everything the way an adult would, instead of a child. That party is very important. Molly's lucky you're the one helping her. Do what you think is best, little angel."

The Big Day

"Mrs. Gemelli? What are you doing here?" Molly put her backpack on the radiator and went into the living room. "Did Amanda go out shopping?"

"Shopping? Oh, my, no. Today was the big day." Mrs. Gemelli straightened the newspapers on her lap and looked over the top of her granny glasses at Molly.

"What big day? And where's Clayton?"

"He went down for a nap right after lunch. He should be up soon if you want to play with him."

"I have homework to do." Molly took out her science sheet and read about the project she was supposed to do. Then she went into the kitchen and found the bag of Popsicle sticks that she'd been collecting for weeks.

Her job was to build an arched bridge out of them that would demonstrate how a keystone worked. The keystone was the wedge-shaped stone at the top of the arch—and it had to fit into the sides perfectly so the whole thing would hold together. They lived in Pennsylvania, which for some reason was called the Keystone State.

The job was hard, because the sticks wouldn't stay in place. The glue simply didn't dry fast enough. Plus, Molly had to break the sticks to certain lengths, but often she broke them too short or too long and had to try again. Finally she finished and put the bridge in a shoe box. It would be safe there until she carried it to school the next day.

Clayton called out from upstairs.

Molly cleaned up the bits of broken Popsicle sticks. Then she emptied her lunch box and put her backpack away.

Clayton was crying now.

"Mrs. Gemelli, Clayton's crying."

28

"He's just exercising his lungs. When he needs me, he'll let me know."

Clayton's cries were getting worse.

Molly went upstairs.

Clayton sat with each hand desperately gripping a bar of the crib. When he saw Molly, though, he smiled right through his tears.

Molly went over, and Clayton lifted his arms to her. "I can't pick you up out of the crib and you know it. You're too heavy for me. You have to scream louder so Mrs. Gemelli will come get you."

Clayton made a little *"ooo"* noise that seemed to circle around the room, like a musical note.

Molly hummed the note herself. Clayton looked at her with an open mouth. A long line of drool hung all the way to his tummy. He was wet and yucky, but he was such a small guy, and in this moment Molly sensed that he felt lonely. "Here." She took the stuffed kangaroo from the corner of the crib and made it hop over to Clayton and jump on his head.

Clayton laughed. Then he pointed at the yellow swan on the bureau.

"Why do you love that swan so much?"

Clayton reached for the swan and gurgled.

Molly went over and picked up the swan. She made it swim in the air all around the crib while Clayton kept gurgling. She made it dive for fish under the mattress. She made it fly to the window and back. Clayton gurgled and gurgled. Molly shook the swan. Clayton laughed at the bell. He reached both hands out and laughed and laughed.

Molly heard the front door open and shut. She put the swan back on the bureau and listened at the door. Amanda and Mrs. Gemelli were talking in the living room now. Molly couldn't make out what they were saying. And then Mrs. Gemelli left.

Amanda came up the stairs in new tan pants and a soft green blouse. "Hi, Molly. And, hello, my best boy." She lifted Clayton out of the crib and hugged and kissed him. "Wow, that's what I call soggy. Someone sure needs a diaper change. Molly, would you sit in the chair with him while I get out of these clothes?"

Molly sat in the chair, and Amanda put Clayton on her lap. Then Amanda dashed off to her room and dashed back a minute later in her usual jeans. She picked up Clayton without a word and carried him over to the changing table.

"Where'd you go?" asked Molly.

"Just out."

"With a boy?"

"Molly, you know, you don't have any right to grill me like this." Amanda finished changing Clayton's diapers and sat down in the chair to nurse him. "In case you didn't notice, I have other things to think about than boys right now."

"Mrs. Gemelli said today was the big day."

"Well it wasn't a big romance day, if that's

what you're thinking." Amanda played with Clayton's ear while he nursed. Her face was all blotchy again. "I haven't gone on a date since Stuart walked away when he found out I was pregnant. I haven't even gone to the movies with girlfriends."

Molly watched Amanda's hand tremble. The room filled with the saddest note in the world. Molly had the urge to hug Amanda. But she wouldn't let herself. "I don't feel sorry for you."

"I didn't ask you to."

"You deserve to be left out. You're the one who caused the problem. I don't deserve it—you do."

"What are you talking about? What don't you deserve?"

"To be left out."

"Who's leaving you out, Molly?"

"Kids' parents don't want me around."

"Oh, Molly. I didn't know." A big tear rolled down Amanda's cheek and clung to her top lip. She licked it off. "No wonder you hate me."

"I don't hate you," Molly mumbled. "Where did you go today, anyway?"

"I took my test."

"What test?"

"What do you think I've been studying for every night? The GED. It's sort of a high school equivalency test. If I pass, I can graduate at the same time as the rest of my class. Then I can go part-time to community college next year."

"Oh." So that's what Amanda had been doing as she gobbled up the cookies at night, curled in the big living room chair with her toes beating out the rhythms on her CDs and a book in her lap. Those were school books. She was studying all that time. "Did they make you buy a new outfit to take the test?" The heat of injustice warmed Molly's chest. "That's so unfair. You had to work hard for that money."

"They didn't care what I wore. I could have taken the test in jeans."

"So why'd you buy that new outfit?"

"I hoped it would help me." Amanda gave a small laugh. "I figured if I looked good, I might do better. You know—have more confidence."

"You looked great," said Molly.

"Thanks."

Angel Talk

M olly's come a long way," said the Archangel of Compassion.

"I guess my job is done, then," said the little angel.

"Oh, no, it's not. You're the one who recognized the anger in the air. There's still plenty of it around," said the archangel.

"There is? Molly seems to be forgiving Amanda. And she was actually playing with Clayton, so even though she may not like him, she's being kinder to him."

"Wait a minute. You're the one who pointed out that there are more people in Molly's world than just Amanda and Clayton," said the archangel. "Did you forget about them?"

The Little Angel of Compassion remembered how Molly wouldn't get in line for a turn on the swing sets because Beth was there. And how Molly wouldn't sit on the bus near Celia that morning. She was closing herself off from the people at school. She was making herself miss out on fun.

And now the Little Angel of Compassion remembered that other little angel who had quit her task—the one who sat all alone and didn't play any of the games at field day.

"Anger isn't always easy to recognize," said the little angel.

The Archangel of Compassion took the little angel's hand. "That's the truth, all right."

Sleep Overs

Molly sat with her back against the sycamore tree. She watched Celia jump rope with a group of girls. Celia hadn't asked her to join them.

Well, it wasn't exactly like that. In fact, it was pretty complicated. Molly had sat by Harry on the bus again this morning. The seat next to him was always empty because no one else liked his grunts. Molly didn't like his grunts, either. But Harry had actually been nice to her today. When she sat down beside him, he opened his lunch box and gave her a powdered doughnut. Anyway, Celia had looked at her funny as they got off the bus. Then at lunch, Celia had saved a seat for Molly. But Molly said she had to eat fast and do something else. So she took a seat near the door and wolfed down her sandwich. Then she went upstairs to the bathroom on the south wing and hid till lunchtime was over. She half-expected to find Sasha in the bathroom, but she wasn't there.

Now it was afternoon recess. Celia had taken one look at Molly, and then gone on outside to the playground without a word. Celia knew Molly wouldn't play with her. So that's why she hadn't asked her.

Molly understood all this. But she still wished Celia had asked her. She looked away, toward the houses on the other side of the school yard fence. She felt like walking over, climbing the fence, and going home.

"Hi, Molly."

Molly turned her head. "Oh, hi, Sasha."

"How come you're sitting over here?"

Molly pulled up a handful of grass and dumped the blades in her lap. "I don't know."

Sasha sat on the ground beside Molly. "It's kind of nice here. Quiet and peaceful. And it's shady. This summer's going to be hot. That's what my mom says."

Thinking of summer made Molly think of the swimming pool. "Are you going to the swim party?" she blurted out. What a stupid question. Sasha was Beth's friend; of course she was going.

"Yup."

Molly took a deep breath. "I'm not."

"I know." Sasha examined her fingernails. "I'm not going to the sleep over afterward, though."

"Why not?" asked Molly.

"You know. My condition and all. If I had an accident and anyone found out, it would be awful."

"Oh." Molly pulled up more grass.

"No one knows but you."

"Not even Beth?"

"Not even Beth."

"It must be terrible to keep a secret like that from your best friend," said Molly.

"It is."

"So why don't you tell her?"

Sasha worked at cleaning the dirt out from under her thumbnail. "She might think I was, I don't know, icky."

"But it's not your fault. You can't help it."

Sasha stood up. "You're brave, Molly. Maybe I'll tell Beth. But I won't go to the sleep over no matter what. I don't want everyone else to know."

Molly stood up, too. Then she realized something. "You've never been to a sleep over, have you?"

Sasha shook her head.

"Well, how about coming to my house Saturday night?"

"Really?" said Sasha. "I could bring a sleeping bag."

"Sure. We could even sleep on the back porch and look at the stars all night."

"Sounds good."

Angel Talk

he Little Angel of Compassion blew a slow, lazy tune on her harmonica. When she finished, she smiled at the archangel.

"That's a beautiful tune," said the archangel.

"Thanks. I was ready to play whatever note Molly needed, but then she came through on her own, without any music from me. So I played this song as a celebration." The little angel played another refrain.

"There is, indeed, a lot to celebrate," said the Archangel of Compassion.

"Molly's not alone anymore." The little angel wiped off her harmonica and put it away. "She let herself be friendly again. And Sasha might turn out to be a good friend."

"Yes. But it's not enough. She misses Celia."

"I know," said the little angel. "Don't worry. I'm not about to stop till I've helped Molly overcome her anger."

Skating

The phone rang. Molly put her name at the top of her science homework and ran to answer it. "Hello?"

"Hi, Molly. My mom's taking me to the skating rink. Want to come?"

Molly loved skating. She almost said yes. Then she thought about the swim party on Saturday—about how Celia was going even though she knew Molly wasn't invited. "I've got things to do, Celia." A blast of harmonica covered most of Molly's words. She jumped back from the phone. "Did you do that?"

"Of course not. What was it?"

"I don't know. I've been hearing harmonica music for days."

"How weird," said Celia. "So what do you say?"

"Maybe I do need some exercise."

"Good," said Celia. "Go ask your sister if you can come."

"She'll say yes." Molly hesitated. Then she added, "She's nice like that."

"I know," said Celia. "We'll pick you up in a few minutes."

Molly put all her stuff away and walked around the house looking for Amanda. "Oh, there you are."

Amanda was sitting on the floor in Clayton's room. She rolled him a big fuzzy ball. Clayton sat with both arms out-stretched. As the ball came to him, he seemed to bounce up off his bottom and throw himself over it. He laughed and bit the ball.

"Celia's mom is taking us to the skating rink."

"Oh, good." Amanda scrambled to her feet and hugged Molly. "Good for you."

Molly put her arms around Amanda's waist

and breathed in the sweet smell of her body lotion. Roses. "Celia's mom has always been nice to me. It's Beth's mom who hates me."

"*Oooo,*" said Clayton. He held on to Amanda's jeans and pulled himself to standing.

"Wow. I didn't know you could stand," Molly said to Clayton.

"He's been doing it all day." Amanda hoisted Clayton onto her hip. "Poor Beth."

"Huh?" Molly stepped back. "Why poor Beth?"

"Think about what it would be like to live with her mother." Amanda rubbed her cheek on the top of Clayton's head. "I hope you never live with anyone full of hate, my funny boy."

Molly stood on tiptoe and kissed Amanda's cheek. "You really are smart, you know. You'll pass that test you took."

"Maybe. I never was very good at tests." Amanda pulled at her eyebrow and looked worried. "Well, go have a good time."

Molly ran downstairs and grabbed her Rollerblades. By the time she went out the door, Celia's car was waiting at the curb. They drove to the rink with the radio blaring. Celia's mom loved to have the radio blaring when she drove. She said that way the noise of kids couldn't drive her nuts. It worked, because the music was so loud, they gave up on trying to talk. Molly rolled down her window and lifted her face to the rushing wind. The happy zing of the music was infectious. Molly let her body move to the rhythms. Maybe that's why Amanda listened to music as she studied; maybe it made her happy.

At the rink Celia's mom headed for the bleachers, where all the other grown-ups sat reading and talking. Celia and Molly sat on the bench and put on their Rollerblades. Molly moved close to Celia. It was good to finally be with her again.

"Oh, no," said Celia. "There's Beth and her mother."

Molly looked up. Beth was on the bench across from them, talking to her mom. Sasha sat right beside them and she was looking straight at Molly.

Beth's mom got up and went over to the bleachers.

Molly felt little pinpoints of excitement all over her skin. She stood up and rolled across to stand in front of Sasha. "Hi."

"Hi, Molly." Sasha gave a big smile.

Beth looked at Molly. Then she looked at her mother over on the bleachers. But her mother was busy talking to someone.

A high, reedy, nervous note tickled Molly's ears. "Hi, Beth."

"Hi." She turned to Sasha. "Let's skate."

"Beth . . ." Molly rolled back and forth in an arc. "My sister took a test, to try to graduate high school. She studied at night. Every night. And she works on Saturday at the grocery."

"Oh." Beth just looked at Molly.

Molly stared straight ahead. It was so hard

to say these things. She wanted to get out on the rink and roll away from everything hard. But she hadn't finished yet—she still had to say the most important thing of all: "My sister's a good mother."

"Amanda's a good person," said Celia, who was standing half behind Molly. "And so is Clayton."

"Just like Molly," said Sasha.

Molly couldn't believe her ears. She swallowed to keep back tears.

Beth looked at all of them. "That's good," she said quietly.

"Let's all skate together," said Sasha. "All of us holding hands."

"All the other skaters will get annoyed with us," said Celia.

"Who cares?" said Molly.

Beth nodded. "Who cares."

Angel Talk

eth's going to be in hot water with her mother," said the Little Angel of Compassion.

"Probably," said the archangel.

"Well, it's about time she stood up to her," said the little angel.

"Wait a minute. Don't go getting involved in Beth's life right now. You're Molly's little angel."

"But Beth needs help, too," said the Little Angel of Compassion.

"You can't be with both of them at once, little angel. And you can't really understand a child well enough to be of help if you don't stick close enough to see everything that's going on." The Archangel of Compassion took the little angel's hand. "I know you want

49

to help everyone, but finish helping Molly first."

The little angel took out her harmonica. "I'm ready."

A Better Day

"Molly, come sit with me." Celia tapped the empty seat beside her.

The seat beside Harry was empty, too, of course. He was looking out the bus window. But he didn't fool Molly at all. She knew he was waiting to see what she'd do.

Molly smiled. She was prepared for this. She sat down beside Harry. "Move over a bit, would you?"

Harry looked astonished. Then he moved close to Molly.

"No, I mean over toward the window."

Harry moved close to the window.

Molly scootched over close to Harry until she was straddling the bump in the middle of the two seats. "Come on, Celia. There's room for you, too."

Celia came over.

They sat three across.

Molly opened her lunch box. She took out a triple pack of chocolate cupcakes. "See? There's one for each of us." She gave one to Harry and one to Celia and took a big bite out of the last one.

Harry smiled wide. Then he stuffed the whole cupcake in his mouth.

"Gross," said Celia. But she laughed.

Molly rode the rest of the way happy. Things were finally going better. Today was Thursday. All she had to do was live through today, tomorrow, and Saturday until seven P.M. Then the swim party would be over and Molly could forget the sleep over party at Beth's because she'd be having her own sleep over with Sasha.

The day went fine until recess. Molly had to stay inside for a few extra minutes because Mrs. Fiwell asked her to erase the black-boards. By the time she got onto the playground, everyone else was already involved in a game. Both Celia and Sasha were playing soccer—and Beth was in their group.

Molly checked the playground again. Even Harry wasn't alone—he was doing crazy jumps with William from the top of the jungle gym. If the playground monitor caught them, they'd get in trouble. But the playground monitor was busy yelling at the girls in line for the swing.

Molly looked back at the soccer game.

It was one thing to skate with Beth when Sasha suggested it. It was another thing to go up on her own and join a game when Beth was there.

Molly waited a long while. Finally, she walked over and stood at the edge of the game.

Celia kicked her the ball.

Molly kicked it back. But the ball went sideways. Toward Beth.

Beth kicked it.

The game went on.

When the playground monitor blew the whistle for the end of recess, Beth came up to Molly. "Hi, Molly."

"Hi, Beth."

"I talked with my mother last night."

There was something about the way Beth said that. Something about her face. Molly knew what Beth was going to say next.

"She still doesn't want you at our house."

Molly blinked. She shouldn't care about a stupid party. But she did. And now she felt like she was going to fall. Then a strong, warm note of harmonica wrapped itself around her and held her up.

"There's not going to be any food at the swimming pool on Saturday. I told my mother I don't want any food there."

Molly didn't know what to say to that.

"The pool isn't really part of my party," said Beth. "I mean, no one's in charge at the pool."

"Oh," said Molly.

"So anyone can come swim." Beth tilted her head. "You like to swim, don't you?"

"Yes," said Molly.

"Well, then, I'll see you there."

Molly looked at Beth's pinched, worried face and thought of what Amanda had said. It must have been hard for Beth to get her mom to agree that she wasn't in charge of whatever happened at the pool. Molly smiled. "I'll be there."

Angel Talk

"Very fine work, little angel," said the Archangel of Compassion. "Molly's anger toward Celia and Beth is finally gone."

The little angel laughed. "Just one more thing, and I think Molly will be able to handle things on her own."

"Really? It looks to me like your wings are thickly feathered already."

"I haven't heard that bell yet," said the Little Angel of Compassion. "And I know exactly the bell I really want to hear."

The archangel smiled quizzically. "I can't wait to find out. Onward, little angel."

The Swan

Molly walked in the front door and knew immediately that something was wrong. Clayton was crying upstairs, and Amanda was crying in the living room.

Molly dropped her backpack on the floor and went into the living room. "What happened?"

"I called for my test results. You can call if you want them early. It only costs six dollars. Otherwise you have to wait for weeks." Amanda wiped both cheeks at once. "I failed."

"Oh, Amanda." Molly sat on the armrest of Amanda's chair and pulled her sister's head to her chest. She hugged her hard. "I'm so sorry."

"And I failed by only two points. Just two lousy points!"

A fighting tune played by the harmonica

marched around Molly. "Can you take it again?"

"Yeah, but I'm just not good at tests."

"You'll pass next time. Start studying right away," said Molly. "And I'll help you."

Amanda pulled back and smiled up at Molly. "You're so silly. How could you help me with high school work?"

"Well, every night when you study, you can make a list of the things you've learned. Then the next night, for the first few minutes I can quiz you on the things you studied the night before. How's that sound?"

"Great." Amanda shook her head. "That's really great, Molly." She stood up. "I'd better go get Clayton. Poor little guy. He woke up when I was on the phone, and then I burst into tears and I couldn't let him see me like that. He's been crying for ten minutes, at least."

"I'll come up, too," said Molly. "In just a minute."

Molly ran to the kitchen and opened the

drawer with the sewing stuff. She took out a needle and threaded it with yellow thread. Then she grabbed a pair of scissors and went upstairs.

Amanda was tickling Clayton's belly as she changed him.

Molly went straight to the bureau and took down the swan. Then she cut off the bell.

Amanda glanced over at her. "What are you doing?"

"You'll see." Then Molly laughed. "I mean, you'll hear." She snipped a hole in the seam on the swan's stomach and pushed in the bell. Then she brought it over to Amanda. "I could sew it myself, but I'd probably make a mess of the stitches. Will you sew it up?"

Clayton let out a little happy scream. He reached for the swan.

Amanda set Clayton on the floor, and Molly sat down beside him. Then Amanda sewed up the hole and handed the swan to Molly.

Clayton bounced on his bottom and gurgled.

Molly made the swan swim all around Clayton's head. Then she handed it to Clayton and kissed him on the cheek.

He shook the swan. *Ring ring ring*. Then he bit it.

Angel Thoughts

The newest Archangel of Compassion blew a parting note of joy on her harmonica to Molly and Amanda and Clayton. Then she flew off in a hurry. She knew a little angel who was probably still sitting alone, and she understood now that that little angel probably didn't want to be alone at all. There were so many games they could play together. The archangel couldn't wait to find out which one the little angel would choose first.

№ 14

Happy Holidays

Sunlight reflected off the snow, making everything more brilliant. The passing cars looked newer, the people's clothes seemed snappier, even the bricks of the buildings took on a richer hue. The world was a better place after a snowfall—that's all there was to it. The Little Angel of Happiness strolled along the freshly shoveled sidewalk, taking it all in with a grin.

Across the street at the tiny train station a group of adults stood on the train platform. A couple of them read newspapers. A few others chatted in little groups. And still others simply waited patiently, seeming to enjoy the bright, cold day as much as the little angel.

But one man definitely wasn't enjoying himself. He patted his vest pocket and felt all his other pockets and rifled through his brief-case. Now he walked in a circle, looking at the ground.

The Little Angel of Happiness recognized the opportunity. He scanned the ground. Nothing. He crossed the street and went along the sidewalk that led up to the train station. It didn't take long for his efforts to be rewarded: A pair of reading glasses in a black case lay at the very edge of the walk, half on the concrete, half in the snow.

The train pulled into the station. The man was bent over, searching under the bench beside the platform. But now he stood up and looked at the train with a face full of resigna-tion.

The little angel ran as fast as he could and placed the glasses case in the man's path as he walked to the train.

The man's mouth opened in surprise. With a smile of satisfaction, he put it in his vest pocket and climbed onto the train.

The Little Angel of Happiness took a deep, happy breath. There was nothing better than starting out the day with a gift that made someone smile. He wandered over to the bench and sat down.

A discarded newspaper lay there. The headlines told of a storm on the way. It was forming way, way up, near the Arctic Circle, but if it did what the forecasters expected, it would be here in a couple of days. The temperature would plummet, and another foot of snow would drop. The little angel put his elbows on his knees and rested his chin in his palms. Winter storms brought so many problems for so many people. His eyes clouded over with worry.

"Good morning." The Archangel of Happiness pushed the newspaper to one side and sat down near the little angel. "I saw that maneuver with the lost glasses. Very nice."

"Thanks." The little angel gave a brief smile.

"You don't seem happy. What's the matter?"

The little angel almost started talking about the storm, when he noticed the piece of paper in the archangel's hand. It had an address written on it. "Who lives there?"

"Oh, just someone or other. No one you'd be interested in." The Archangel of Happiness crossed his legs and leaned back on the bench. He gave a phony yawn.

The little angel smiled. "You're teasing me, aren't you? I bet that's the address of a child. You've got a task for me."

"What do you know, you're wearing a smile again. You do know about happiness." The archangel laughed. "I guess you are the right little angel for this task, after all. The child who lives at this address needs a lot of help learning to find delight in the world."

The little angel jumped off the bench in excitement. "The winter holidays are starting soon. If I help this child and earn enough feathers to get my wings, I can fly through the holidays."

"Now that's a nice goal," said the archangel. "But, more importantly, if you're successful, the child will be able to open her heart to the joys of the season."

The little angel gave a small smile of apology. "You're right. That is more important." Then he tilted his head playfully. "Still, among all the bells of this holiday season, it'll be thrilling to hear my own special bell—the bell that will ring when I get my wings."

The archangel laughed again. He handed the little angel the slip of paper. "You're good at finding addresses. Want to lead the way?"

Macaroni and Cheese

What was that smell? Raquel peeked in the oven. Baked macaroni and cheese. But it wasn't ready yet, and Raquel was hungry.

She stamped her foot. Nothing happened, because no one was around to hear it. So she wandered into Grandma and Grandpa's room.

"Beautiful day, isn't it?" said Grandma. She stood at the window and didn't even turn around. Old people were supposed to have poor hearing, but not Raquel's grandparents. All Raquel had to do was open her door a crack, and Grandma would greet her. "Would you like to help me?"

Raquel came up beside Grandma.

Grandma handed her a miniature spade. "I think this narcissus over here, the third one from the end, is going to bloom today. If you just loosen up the dirt a couple of inches out from the bulb, that might help."

The row of ten narcissus bulbs in the aluminum flower box stood straight and evenly spaced, like drummers in a parade. Raquel poked the little spade into the dirt, when she happened to look out the window.

Hector was clumping along the sidewalk with a huge blue plastic saucer slung over his shoulder. He wore a big grin and looked like he was talking to himself. Maybe he was singing. Raquel just bet he was going to the sledding hill at the elementary school. If it weren't so cold, she'd open the window and ask him.

"I want a blue saucer," said Raquel.

"A blue saucer? You mean a teacup and saucer?"

"No, a sledding saucer."

"Don't you have a new sled?" asked Grandma. "Your father bought it for your birthday. It's the same shape as the toboggan I had as a girl."

"Who cares?" Raquel jammed the spade into the dirt so that it stood there on its own. "I want one like Hector's. It's better than mine. No, I want one bigger than Hector's." She brushed off her hands, even though they weren't dirty, and went back into the kitchen.

Mommy was just taking the casserole of macaroni out of the oven.

Raquel got a plate and sat at the table.

Mommy put a sandwich on Raquel's plate.

"I want macaroni and cheese."

"That's for my cookie group's luncheon," said Mommy. "I made you tuna fish."

Raquel could just imagine all those mothers sitting around talking and laughing as they ate like pigs. "They get the good stuff and I get junk?"

"Be glad I'm going to this cookie luncheon," said Mommy. "We all baked ten dozen of our favorite cookies and we're exchanging them, with the recipes. I'll come home with a dozen each of ten different kinds of cookies. And if you really love any of them, I'll have the recipe so I can make more."

"I hate cookies."

"Don't be silly. You gobble cookies up. And now we'll be set for the holidays. No more baking."

"You'll be set," said Raquel. "I never bake, anyway." Something green stuck out from inside Raquel's sandwich. She lifted a corner of the bread and peeked. "You put olives in here. The ones with the red stuff in the middle."

"They taste so good. And don't they look pretty? And seasonal." Mommy gave a happy sigh as she put her casserole into a carry-bag.

The sandwich didn't smell anywhere near as good as the casserole. Raquel went and sat under the stairs.

Grandpa walked by. "Raquel, is that you under the stairs again?"

"Yes."

"Down in the dumps, huh? What is it this time?"

"Mommy made macaroni and cheese for the women at her luncheon," said Raquel, "and Hector has a new blue sledding saucer."

"Oh." Grandpa just stood there.

"They're happy," said Raquel. "They have good things. All I have is tuna fish. And I hate green olives with red stuff."

Grandpa reached in his pocket. "Breath mint?"

Raquel looked at the little roll of breath mints helplessly. Only Grandpa would make such a yucky offer. She wrinkled her nose. "I hate everything."

Don't miss these other *Aladdin Angelwings* stories!